TODD'S BED TIME STORIES

(VOLUME ONE)

by

Mr. Clark Dillon Jr

DORRANCE
PUBLISHING CO
EST. 1920
PITTSBURGH, PENNSYLVANIA 15238

Dorrance Publishing Co
585 Alpha Drive
Pittsburgh, PA 15238
Visit our website at www.dorrancebookstore.com

ISBN: 978-1-4809-9621-2
eISBN: 978-1-4809-9601-4

TODD'S BED TIME STORIES

"Can you tell me a scary story tonight?" he asked, softy swaddling him-self tightly in my fur.

I held him close and said, "Oh no. No more scary stories for you. It's too late, my son."

"I promise I won't be scared this time! Please. Please tell me!"

He kept staring at me real heard with his big brown eyes, and I re-ally didn't want to hear him whine.

"Very well then, Peter. I'll try to tell a story, but it's not going to be scary."

He was too excited. He sat up straight, crossing his legs and backed up a little.

"This story is about a little girl. Maybe just a few years older than you. She lived with her parents in a different time, on the far side of the world."

FORGOTTEN IN THE WHITE

"ROSE, DON'T FORGET TO BRUSH YOUR TEETH BEFORE YOU COME DOWN!" Mommy yelled from downstairs.

With my mouth full of tooth paste and a toothbrush in my hand, I yelled back, "I know Mommy!" Taking my final spit, I rinsed out my mouth and ran downstairs.

Mommy was in the kitchen cleaning up from breakfast earlier; Dad must have already left because I didn't see him down here.

"Okay good, you're here. Go get in the car. I'm just going to get my coat and shoes, and I'll be right out there," she said.

"Okay," I replied. I went through the garage door and got in the back seat of the car. I really didn't feel like going to the store today. I wish I was old enough to stay here by myself. I put on my seat beat and tried to predict how many stores we were going to go to today.

After a minute or two, Mommy got in the car and backed out the drive way. It was very cold out, but with the snow everywhere, it looked really pretty out. Every-thing was covered in snow, and it made it all sparkle and twinkle, like we were driving through millions of stars. It was snowing out, but just a little. I was looking at all the houses as we drove past. It looked like a wolf was in between two houses watching us drive by. It was hard to see because it was white, but it was staring right at me.

"Mommy, you should have seen it. It was a wolf or fox, but it was looking right at me," I said trying to get her attention.

"I don't think so, Rose, there's no wolves out here. But I was thinking maybe we should hit Kroger first, then go to Walmart for what we don't find at Kroger. Because Kroger is closer," she said back, changing the subject. I kept looking out the window and that opened up the floor for her to talk some more. I wasn't really listening. Instead I was drawing on the window and watching all the light, bright snow gently falling from the sky.

The roads were very slippery and caused everyone on the street to drive slowly, so it felt like it took forever just to get to Kroger. Arriving at the store, Mommy pulled up recklessly into a parking spot. The cold windy air hit face hard. The sky was completely gray, and cars were constantly driving in and out of the parking lot.

Mommy grabbed my hand, and we started walking towards the store. Red tail lights lit deep in the lot as the bright piercing head lights made its way through the falling snow. Mommy got a basket, and we went straight for the fruits first. The whole time while we were in the store, I was always holding onto her. If not her hand, then her coat. She wanted me to stay close at all time because there were always so many people here, and she didn't want me to get lost.

Despite the weather, there were a lot of people there that day, too. People rushing in and out, no one reading the signs above, so they were looking for certain items in the wrong aisle, and old impatient woman waiting in long lines at the front end of the store. I never understood why there would be a thousand people in the store and only a couple registers open. I knew it was only a matter of time before it was us waiting in those long lines.

After searching aisle after aisle, Mommy's phone started to ring.

"Hi babe, is everything okay?" She answered the phone. After a few seconds she responded, "Yes I will. (Pause.) I'll leave right after Kroger, dear."

She put the phone back in her purse and sighed.

"Is everything okay, Mommy?" I asked, still attached to her coat.

"Yes baby. Daddy called and told me that we have to go straight home after this store. He said it's really bad outside, and we shouldn't be out. So looks like we can't make it to Walmart today."

MR. CLARK DILLON JR

Of course, I was happy about not going to Walmart, but I wondered where Daddy was since it was so bad out. Mommy grabbed a few more things, then walked back to the front of the store to get in line. The line was very long, and through the windows, I could see how hard and fast the snow was coming down.

"Look Mommy. Look how fast the snow is coming down," I said, pointing out towards the window.

She looked in the direction where I was pointing and said, "Wow, Rose, it's getting pretty bad out there. We need to hurry up and get home."

More lanes started to open up, so the line got shorter, and we were able to get out the store within a reasonable time. We tried to carry all the bags ourselves to the car, and it was a bad idea. The wind was blowing extremely harshly, which made it difficult to walk. Struggling to walk forward, it got harder to carry all the bags. It got darker out, like really dark. It looked like it was 9:00 at night, but it was only about noon.

Once we got to the car, Mommy took the bags from and put them in the trunk. The wind was throwing so much snow all over the place, it become impossible to see. Lights from the cars continued to shine but then, *CRASH!* I heard a car slam into another. My mother screamed, and then another car came spinning out of control towards us.

As I screamed for my life, Mommy picked me up and jumped to the side. The spinning car collided with ours. It just missed us. With us laying on the parking lot, we heard several more car crashes. Mommy kept asking if I was okay and touching my face and body. I was so scared, but I answered, letting her know that I was okay. People were arguing and yelling at each other in the street and in the parking lot. I couldn't see anything, but I could hear them yelling about everyone crashing. I was freezing to death and didn't know what to do. Mommy was still on the ground, and I was on top of her. It looked like she was trying to get up but she kept moaning in pain.

"Mommy, Mommy, are you okay? Are you hurt?" I asked sliding off her stomach.

"I'm okay, Rose, I just landed on my back," she said trying to stand herself up. She held my hand, and we were going to go back in the store for a minute.

When we got back inside, there were so many more people here, the store was almost full. We had to stop at the entrance (inside) and stand off to the side. Mommy pulled out her phone to call Daddy.

"Anthony! Anthony, we're still at Kroger. It's too dangerous to drive, and there are cars everywhere. A car almost hit us!" She explained, panicking. Mommy had to sit down because her back was hurting. While she was talking to Daddy on the phone, the power shut off and came back on. Everyone in the store gasped as the power blinked on and off and on again. I sat down in Mommy's lap, and we watched everyone as she held me close.

"I told Daddy that we're okay, and once it gets safe out, he'll come and get us." Mommy said. Other families stayed together as well. The employees of the store walked around making sure everyone was okay.

"Mommy, I'm scared." I said, watching all those around me.

"It's going to be okay, sweetie," she said, kissing my forehead.

I kept looking around at everyone. Little kids stayed close to their parents, many people sat up and down the aisles, and guys were always going in and out of the restrooms. It was mostly quiet with mainly the storm outside being the loudest. Some people talked in small groups. The families next to us talked about a plane that crashed during the storm. Some were saying that the storm came out of nowhere and that it shouldn't have hit us.

Time continued on, but the storm didn't let up. These scared stranded minutes turned into hours. Daddy called a few more times, but the storm kept him trapped at home. I had to use the restroom, but I didn't want to get up. Mommy was really starting to get really worried. She kept asking me if I was okay and if needed anything. We would look out the window together and watch all the snow come down. It was so bad out, you couldn't really see all the cars crashed all over the place. The people in the store became uneasy. Some people were stealing food and hiding it with their families. Some of the employees noticed but were too afraid to say anything. Two people walked in from the back of the store and spoke out to gain everyone's attention. The one talking kind of looked like he worked in here.

"I am truly sorry, people. I really am. But we have to leave the building immediately. The storm has severally damaged some electrical panels and other areas of the store. It is now too dangerous to stay here in the store. So we need to work together to get everyone and everything and start exiting the store," the man said to all.

Some mumbled and complained amongst themselves and others spoke out in anger.

"What do you mean leave the building? There is nowhere else to go!" a man shouted.

"It is no longer safe here, sir. We all must leave I'm sorry," the employee said back.

"This is insane! It's too cold and too dark to be out. We won't make it out there!" a woman yelled as she stood up. My mother held me tighter.

Before the man was able to reply to her, another person stood up to speak out of anger, "How dangerous is this place? Because there isn't anywhere to go out there for miles. I mean we have children here! They won't be able to make it out there. You'll be killing us all if you force us all out into the cold."

"I get what you all are saying. It sounds crazy, and I know you're afraid. You don't want to go into the dark. But we don't have a choice. We have to get out of here, and we need to leave now. Stick together and help the women and children. We can do this," he said loudly. He was very clear on leaving, and when he was done talking, he started helping others off the floor. The employees were helping people and guiding them towards the exits. I helped Mommy get up, but I could tell she was in real pain. She held me so close to her, and we joined the crowd of people slowly walking towards the doors.

The wind from outside rushed in and everyone moaned as the cold air wrapped around us all. It was pitch black outside, with nothing but the light of the store to brighten the ferocious snow. We got closer and closer to door. Other kids around me wrapped their faces and smaller ones were carried by the parents. I felt extremely bad for the infants; I was worried that they would die in the cold. Women cried as they got closer to the door. But their tears froze before they fell off her their faces. Once it was our turn to step into the darkness, Mommy made sure I wasn't going to leave her side. I held on to my mother with all my life; I had never felt more afraid and colder in my life. People up head used their phones and anything that could glow for light. It was so cold, oh my God. The wind knocked over the elderly, the weak; some tried to help them up, but the cold kept everyone focusing on themselves.

"Don't let go of my hand!" Mommy said.

I was too cold to respond. I was barely able to walk. Together as group we all started walking. I think we were walking home. People were falling down and falling behind. My legs become so weak. I was slowing down. Mommy noticed, and she stopped and picked me up. We weren't walking as fast, but I was so much warmer. Leaning over her shoulder, I watched the people behind us. They were struggling badly and I felt horrible just watching them. People were falling over and not getting back up. A giant gust of wind blew and knocked everyone over. Everyone screamed, including me. I wanted to scream some more and call out for Mommy, but I was too cold.

I rolled over and grabbed her. She was out cold. I kept shaking, her but she wouldn't wake up. I tried calling her name, but she still didn't respond. Everyone else was trying to get and carry their family. It looked like a lot of people were knocked out.

The wind blew harder. The snow turned into ice. It also started hailing. Big chunks. It was starting to get harder to see because the lights were scattered everywhere, and the falling snow become too thick. It was getting so bad out that people started walking back towards the store. I didn't know what to do; I couldn't have been more scared in my life. I finally got strong enough to call out for help. A few times, I screamed help but no one came. I guess no one heard my shaky, frozen voice. People continued to walk away. My head was killing me because the hail was so big. I leaned over my mother and tried to make sure she didn't get hit.

"Ahahahaha!" Someone yelled from a distance. Then I heard another yell from someone closer. Through all the wind and hail, I kept hearing people scream and crying out for help. It sounded like they were being attacked. These were screams of death. The screams were getting closer.

I started shaking Mommy again, but still no movement from her. I raised my head, and standing in front of me was a giant animal. Staring right into my eyes, the creature had beautiful ocean blue eyes. It just stood there growling at me, showing its sharp teeth and staring at me. All I could see was the blue from its eyes and the blood dripping from its mouth. I was frozen solid, but I wanted to help my mom. I tried to cry, but it was too cold.

With all the fear in me, I yelled, "Help me!"

It stopped growling instantly. Using its paws, it curled my mother and rested around her. It looked like a fox. One of its paws reached out and pulled me in. It sat me down, and I rested under its comfortable fur. I was warm, and I grabbed my mother's hand. Not the chill from the wind nor the ice from the snow touched me. The blood from the animal mouth dripped softly onto my coat.

Once the hail stopped, the creature slid my mother onto its back. It leaned down just low enough for me to climb onto it. I got on and grabbed onto its fur. I stayed low in the fur because it was so warm. It started walking swiftly towards my house.

We passed plenty of people on the way there. People were laid out all over the street and sidewalks. They must have passed out or died from the cold. It was still very dark and hard to see. We started to slow down and then eventually we came to a complete stop. We were on my front lawn, and the house was completely buried under snow. There was no way in.

The creature took a deep breath and blew. It blew a soft wind that pressed all the snow to the side, clearing a path to the front door. I jumped off its back and ran to the front door, but it was locked. I knew Mommy had the key on her somewhere, but the fox rubbed the door knob, and it opened. It walked in and laid Mommy on the couch.

Once I got in, I closed the door and ran upstairs, looking for Daddy. I checked all the rooms, but he wasn't here. I ran back downstairs to Mommy. Laying there on the couch she was still as stone. I didn't know why she wouldn't wake up.

The massive creature stood firm behind me.

I turned to face it and said, "Thank you."

I reached up to wrap both my arms around its neck and hugged it with all the strength I had left.

"You're welcome, Rose," it said with its deep voice, raising one leg around me and hugging me back.

I stepped backwards in all and said, "You can talk?"

It walked over to Mommy and gently kissed her on the forehead.

"I will bring your father back to you, child. Do not leave this house," the great animal commanded. I nodded my head yes, and it walked out the front door and closed it behind itself.

As soon as he left, my mother began to awake. I hugged her stomach hard, and she said, "Oh, Rose, not so tight. Where are we?" She moaned a little more and looked around as she tried to sit herself up.

"We're home, Mommy. A giant fox saved us." I said excited.

"What are you talking about? Rose, what happened?" she said again.

"You're not going to believe me, so when he comes back with Daddy, you'll see for yourself," I said sitting down on the floor next to her.

She mumbled to herself a little more then she said, "Where's your father?"

$$\bowtie$$

Before I could continue on with the story, Peter had fallen asleep. I pulled the blanket over him and watched him as he snored lightly. I laid down around him and closed my eyes.

"Good night, Todd."

"Good night, Peter."

THE END

MR. CLARK DILLON JR

BURNING RED

CHAPTER 1

I WATCHED HIM BURN; he burned right in front of me. His flesh boiled, and he screamed louder than life. I could feel his pain. I could hear his cry as he shouted out to God. The creatures led me to watch my father burn before my eyes. Fire, brimstone, and devastation filled the black darkness around us.

After a few minutes, the screaming stopped; the man before me wasn't my father any more. The man was nothing more than an empty figure. A faceless figure, a figure without a soul. I often wondered what my father had done to get him and his son beaten and taken to a place just to set the man on fire. But now I was here, no father, no mother, and no friends. I was lost. Lost in the city, the city of sorrow.

As I balled up my fist, my veins raged heavily against my flesh, and one thought floated around in my head. I would be feared and respected; everyone would know my name, then I would strike and take revenge on the monsters who took my father away from me.

I bit the rope; the rope fell slowly to the dark wooden floor. But I walked even slower to the faceless figure. I raised my hand to touch the figure, but I wasn't strong enough. I dropped to my knees and wanted to cry, but I had no tears. I tried to speak, but I had no words, I was only 11 but my life had just begun for the first time.

The door opened. I turned around quickly, and one of the creatures had come back. One of them was a big, dirty black man. The man approached me and said, "I hope you understand that this wasn't personal."

His words were no comfort to me. I wanted nothing but to see him burn like my father did. A rage lit within me that could never be put out. A fire that hungered for revenge. I wanted these monsters to pay for what they had done, and I wouldn't rest until they got what they deserved.

I didn't understand; nothing I did seemed to work. I couldn't escape the pain. I just couldn't see a way out. It's like the side of the moon we'll ever see, or the flower you'll never see bloom. I just didn't see a life where I wasn't smothered in this burning hate. The image of the figure burning repeatedly reminded me every day. This so-called "father figure" told me I must mask my pain and find a way to move on. Typical. Anyone trying to give advice would say that.

As time passed, I only grew angrier. I saw these ungrateful kids disrespecting their parents, and it sickened my soul. I never knew my mother, never saw her before in my life. My father was beaten and burned right in front of me. These children had no idea how lucky there really were. I wished there was something to do. I usually stayed at home and did my work or went down to the park to play ball. But it wasn't enough. There was a hole in my soul. A vast hole that was expanding. I tried serval things to fill it, but none of them worked.

Of course, the first thing I tried was weed because it was so easy to get where I was. The weed was only a temporary escape. While riding a panda, my problems would be no more. The fact that I had no mother, no father... nothing bothered me anymore. I didn't care about anything. Nothing existed when I was high, but, like I said before, it was only temporary. I would get off my high, and my problems would come back even harder.

The next thing I tried was sex. But none of those things could fill that void in my soul. This black hole that was expanding was going to continue to expand until it consumed my entire soul. As far as I know it already did.

This world didn't make sense to me. I hated everything about life and living. I wanted nothing to do with this life. Every day got worse. Every year turned me more and more into a monster. Before I knew it, I had become the very thing I hated so much about this world. I had become a monster, just like the ones who destroyed my father. This world was cruel, and if you were not strong enough, you would be destroyed or turned into a product of this life.

CHAPTER 2

I RAN; I RAN AS FAST AS I COULD. I hopped the first fence and cut the corner around the house. They were right on my heels. The bullets zipped passed me and bounced off the ground behind me. Their footsteps stomped loudly as they hunted me down. Their voices raged loudly in the air under the gun fire. My legs started to give out from under me. I couldn't run much longer; I went into someone's driveway and banged on the side door.

"Let me in! Please let me in!"

No one opened the door, but one of those monsters saw me and... He raised his gun and pointed it at me. The fear that flowed through my veins matched the anger that flowed through his veins. Sweat dropped slowly off his hand and onto the floor. Then, he pulled the trigger. Fire shot out the gun, and before I could blink, my body fell and crashed onto the ground. My burning, red blood poured out of my stomach and onto the pavement. The pain was so unbearable, it felt like my insides were on fire. Within a few seconds, everything went black.

❧❧

The young man awoke in an alley not too far from his house. With blood still slowly making its way down his body, like lava flowing down a volcano. He walked, well, more liked crawled back to his house. He opened the door, and his grandmother was laying down on the couch, right where we left her. He stood there and stared at her because, because she was dead. Her mouth hung open, her dull eyes stared at the celling, as her head laid back against the couch.

$$\mathfrak{X}\mathfrak{C}$$

I dropped to my knees. I saw her lifeless shell rotting on the dirty old couch. I looked around for help, and no one was there. I shouted out for help, but no heard me. No one came to my rescue; no one came to her rescue either. She was all I had, and she was gone. I was all alone in this cold, dreadful world. That sweet and wonderful woman was all I had left!

Why stay in a world where love doesn't exists? Where your brothers abandon you at a young age, when your father repeatedly abused you because you were never the son he wanted. I couldn't take it anymore!

I darted into the kitchen and grabbed a knife.

I sat on the floor against the wall under a window. I placed the knife closely to my weak neck. One by one, unfaithful tears rolled down my face. I was never the star child; I was never believed in, but I always told myself that there was always someone out there worse off than me. That thought seemed to make things better, but only for a short period of time. I pressed the knife closer. I was never understood; I was always picked last, last in everything.

But now, now. It all ended here: my pains, weaknesses, and failures would all die with me here. I slammed the knife into my throat, and I choked to death on the knife.

$$\mathfrak{X}\mathfrak{C}$$

MR. CLARK DILLON JR

Fear. Fear is the reason why most people make the choices they do. This young man was beaten, shot, and shot where it hurts him the most. Why have man become the way that they are? Beasts and monsters. Creatures of the dark. Destroyers of their own kind.

The young man needed one thing. Maybe it could have saved his life, but did he even die to start off with? Maybe a little support, maybe a little love, and his story could have been a whole lot different. Blind men are. Men have blinded themselves, and now many people are paying the price! But why should they? This young man did nothing to deserve what happened to him.

Life isn't fair, true, but there is someone who can change that.

CHAPTER 3

THE SCREAMS WERE THE LOUDEST. Everyone around knew that we were going to die.

First, the children. They were sucked out into the lost blueness of the sky. Left to wander the open blue emptiness and eventually plummet to their death. It was a sham that man wasn't given wings to fly. If we could fly, we probably wouldn't have been on this plane in the first place.

I looked at my wife, and she squeezed my hand tightly. In that brief moment, she passed all of her hope into my hand. I looked into her eyes; her bright brown eyes sparkled, giving me a sign of hope. The air pressure... The air was so intense. The air pounded and pressed heavily against me. Someone was holding on to a seatbelt; he was dangling in the air. The hole at the top of the plane was expanding. I looked back at my wife, and her seatbelt snapped loose, and smacked her dead in the face. Burning, red blood shot out her face, and she took off.

"Noooo!" I screamed as I reached for her.

By the grace of God, I caught her hand. I held tight; I held on with all my strength and heart. My soul depended on her, and if she was to go, I would be lost. This was all too much to take in.

She said with her lips, "I love you."

Then her hand slipped right out my mine, and she flew into the sky. I cried! Oh God, I cried! My everything was lost; the plane crashed! I flew out my seat, flipped over the chair in front of me, then I clipped the corner of the bathroom door, and lastly crashed into the wall.

ꝰↄⅭ

The man awoke serval days later in a hospital. With his right leg, left arm, left wrist, six fingers broken. So many of his bones broken. Also, he got a new scar that came down across his face from clipping the door. This man had just lost all the love he ever had. Out of 234 people on that plane, only six of them survived, him being one of that six. This tragedy dominated the news for weeks. No one knows what happen to cause the plane crash, but everyone had their opinions and theories. The man stayed in the hospital for a long time, and when was released, he still was on crutches. When he got home, he couldn't handle the lost and sadness. He couldn't sleep anymore; he had completely lost it. He lost his job and all friends, he started to go crazy.

ꝰↄⅭ

I woke up in the middle of the night from the same dream, again! I couldn't sleep, I couldn't eat. I didn't understand why I couldn't operate. My whole life was taken from me in that plane crash.

Why?! Why did she leave me? The sky took her away from me when I needed her most. I know others lost their families and lives, but they're not me! God, how could he have done this to me? A piece of me had died in that crash, and that piece would never come back. Without it, I was useless and meaningless. I ran outside and stared into the sky. It was a bright and beautiful day, not a cloud in sight. But I saw it differently; the sky was a murderer. I yelled at the sky. I dropped to my knees and cried.

Two cars pulled up in my driveway, one of them happen to be a cop car.

⚸⚸

His old friend and a police officer had taken him to a mental institution.

For weeks, then months, he stayed in there. Every day, the man lost a little more humanity; a little more personality would leave. It was like he was turning into a robot. He didn't interact with any other people. He had become nothing more than nothing. The months turned into years, and it seemed like he was never going to get out. This man had lost everything and felt like there was nothing else to live for. He was nothing short of a miracle, and he wasted his second chance at life by slowly rotting away. That man stayed there for the rest of his life. Eventually his friends stopped visiting him; the doctors stopped trying to help him, and he gave up on everything. He was to spend the remainder of days sealed behind gray walls.

⚸⚸

This morning, I awoke from the same dream I have every night, but this morning was different. A giant white wolf stared at me as I laid in bed with its pitch blue eyes.

"I am a fox. But I understand your confusion, human. I do look a lot like a wolf."

The heavy dark voice came from the creature.

"I have truly lost it. Am I that far gone?" I asked, sliding upwards in the bed to sit up.

"I've watched you human, for a very long time. I felt your pain when you lost the woman you loved. I also felt you die a little every day after her passing. Now you are completely lost, and you are going to spend the remaining of your days here. You have wasted the life, the second chance you were given. Do you think it was by luck that you survived that crash?"

"What a minute. Are you even real? What the hell are you talking about?!" I shouted.

"You were given another chance to do something with your life. He spared your life, and you wasted it! You threw everything away because she died! You were supposed to share your story and provide hope to those who lost it!" the ferocious fox yelled.

He started to growl with anger. I was too scared to move, too scared to react. The fox's ears jumped up, then he paused. He jumped into the wall, and the doctor came into my room immediately after the white creature disappeared. The doctor was with two guards, and he asked me why was I in here shouting.

I tried to tell them about the talking fox, but they didn't believe me. He pulled out a syringe, and the two others began to hold me down. I started shaking and screaming about the talking fox, but everything eventually faded to dark.

THE END

ENCHANTED MEMORY

THE STREETS WERE FILLED WITH FEAR AND VIOLENCE. A thick, hard, gray layer of ash covers and owns the sky. The people raged and fought for control. What pushes a man to this point? What could possibly happen that could turn friends and neighbors against each other. Was it greed? Lies? Disparateness?

The stores were looted before they burned, houses being raided by strangers, the weak killed in the chaos. Even the children took full advantage—they stole anything they could carry and scattered everywhere like rats. Evil and hate stretched from one end of the city to the other. As I looked around, I saw groups of people drag helpless women into corners and down alleys with sexually and devious intent. People were thrown off roof tops; men beaten and stomped to death, cars flipped in the street, and the authorities powerless to stop the madness.

In fact, the authorities had it the worst. The ones that tried to calm this down before it got out of hand were beaten and hung in the streets. Their bodies hung and swayed back and forth in the wind. Inside the buildings and stores, people fought each other for whatever they could get their hands on, using anything as weapon for an advantage. Stabbing each other with broken bottles, house knives, and tools such as screwdrivers. Shooting others without mercy, shotguns blasting and tearing off limps, handhelds piercing flesh, and assault rifles painting bodies red. Once civilized and pure people were now ruthless and relentless creatures of the dark.

The screams and cries filled the atmosphere all around us. You could also hear the sick laughter amongst all the destruction as they enjoyed it. Women cried for the loss of her children. Moans of pain sickened me. The fires burned brighter, giving the chaos a way to see, the streets were flooded with blood as bodies made anywhere their home. It seemed like every person had completely lost all humanity and became something else. Doctors whose sole purpose was to heal had no problem choking and stabbing a man to death; teachers who were supposed tutor and teach drove over children grinding their little bodies under the tires to reach safety. These people couldn't be reasoned with or talked to. Nothing was going to stop these people from burning this city to the ground.

The chaos had reached outside the city and hit the suburbs and neighborhoods. Many people invaded houses up and down the block. Families pulled out from their homes and beaten to death on their front lawn. Dads and husbands beaten brutally to a bloody, slow death as the children watched awaiting their turn.

The corner house seemed to be drawing a lot of attention. Multiple groups of people made their way toward the house. Defenders from inside would spring up at different windows and send bullets flying at invaders. But that didn't stop them from trying to get in. Eventually, they overwhelmed the house and started breaking in from all angles.

Since that family killed so many people that tried to break in, the intruders wanted to make an example. The kids were smacked with rakes and shovels then hung from branches of the trees in the yard. Blood rushed from the top of their heads then dropped softly off their dead, cold feet. The wife was passed around from man to man. Everyone got a chance to know her. The father was quartered in the middle of street after watching all of this happen to his family. The people tied rope to his arms and legs and pulled until it was just a head and torso that dropped on the pavement. They threw his limbs on his body and watched all the blood pour out. This was truly a sad sight to see. There wasn't one person who wasn't fighting, stealing, or killing. This entire city was drowning in its own blood.

I kept waiting for someone to end this. This was going on for entirely too long. This destruction and nonstop killing went on for days. Every day got a little better because after the first three days, most of the people in the city were dead. The city looked like a forgotten war zone. Bodies hung all through the city streets and neighborhoods. Blood stained almost every wall and door, small fires continued to burn and provide light to this dead land.

Days turned into weeks. The city had become a complete ghost town. No one came outside for anything—well, not where you could be seen at least. People were scared and scattered throughout the city. The smell of blood and bodies every-where made it impossible to be anywhere without wearing a mask. People only came out in the dark and when they needed to steal something to survive. More like rats than humans, you can say.

Everything was silent. Nothing but the sound of fires, and hundreds of flies hovering around the bodies. This place will never be the same. Changed forever. There is no more life here; only survival.

THE END

A SINFUL WALK

I CRAWLED OUT OF THE CAR AND STAYED LOW. I checked myself to see if I had been shot. Jay and Lamar had already got out the car and posted up. It was a war zone, nothing but a blood bath. As bullets and cries shot and zipped all around me, the only thing I could hear was Jessica's soft voice saying, "Roy, please don't go. He'll kill you if you do go. Please stay here with me. Hold me, and don't let me go."

The thick gray clouds blocked all hope from leaving this city, my boys shooting out their windows, holding their own. Walker and the others posted up in the park. I peeked around the car, and they were getting closer. I turned back and took a deep breath, pulling out my glock. Lamar's body smacked down onto the pavement right in front of me in a blink of an eye with blood spilling and flowing out his body. I reached out to grab him, but he stepped on my hand. I raised my head to look at him and saw nothing but evil in his eyes. He held a gun to my face and I closed my eyes. Everything went silent, then I opened my eyes again, and he was falling toward me with a chunk of his head missing.

I pushed him over got up and ran to the house across the street. I took cover by the side of the house. Someone started running towards me shooting, but each shot chipped the house. I dove across him, landing on towards his side, then kicked him in the side of his leg. He tripped over, so I quickly got on the top of him and started beating him in the face with the butt of my gun.

Once his face was soaked in blood, I pressed the gun heavily against his left eye. I pulled the trigger, and his thoughts sneezed all over my face. I jumped back up and took cover behind a car in the driveway. My boy Jay saw me and ran to me. Dodging and ducking the hell fire, he got to me.

"I fear we're the last ones. And those bastards won't stop for nothing until we're all dead," he said, trying to keep it together.

Looking back up, I saw everyone in their houses shooting out their windows, those clowns across the street didn't hold anything back. They were just firing back. Then I saw him. Walker, coated in darkness and drenched in anger.

Walker and four others ran up to a house and kicked the door down. They walked in spraying. The fire and light was just bright enough to cast the images of the bodies being torn apart by the gunfire. Blood and fallen souls flew out the window like they were late for an appointment. It seemed like that was all it took.

In small groups, the wild beast ran and invaded the houses, without mercy, without a thought. These lost creatures slaughtered my neighbors, my friends, my people were taken to place where only red is what they could see. This heated place had been calling our number for far too long now, but this isn't the way we should meet our destiny.

Without thinking, I went in the house after one of the groups. I had to stop these niggas from killing us all. I then quickly eliminated them niggas posted up by the windows. I shot one in the back of his head, grabbed another, kicked him in the back of his leg so he dropped to his knees, then sent his brains to think all over the floor.

Jay came up behind me and shot the other two down. I stared at the bodies around me. I felt like I was standing in the middle of hell itself.

"Roy! It's that crazy nigga Walker!" Jay yelled with his voice overwhelmed with fear.

I looked out the window closest to me, hoping it was someone else. My heart pounded against my chest repeatedly. I wiped the sweat off my forehead and onto the floor. Out the window, Walker and two others were running up to the house.

"Kill 'em Jay! Shoot!" I yelled.

One after another, bullets left our guns and headed towards Walker and them. We were too late. The others stayed outside, but Walker crashed into the house and fell up against the wall. He shot Jay four times in throat and face.

MR. CLARK DILLON JR

As Jay's lifeless body slowly fell backwards towards hell, his burning red blood lit up the room. As soon as his body made contact with the floor, Walker looked at me for a second then started letting those bullets fly again.

I ran to the other side of the room listening to the bullets whiz past me. I dove behind the couch.

"I trusted you, Roy! You were my brother!" Walker yelled after firing a few more shells through the couch I was behind. I could hear the sadness in his tone.

The earth was standing still. I was out of ammo for my gun. I had nothing left; I was a man with nothing to lose. I stood up slowly; I turned to face him. He was just standing there, aimed right at me. His whole body was shaking like he saw a ghost. His eyes were bloodshot red, and a few tears ran down his hopeless face.

I dropped the gun and said, "I'm still your brother. I'm still your friend! Walker, you have to believe me. I didn't know. I would never betray you like that. I..."

BAM!

ƆXƆ

The gun shot one last bullet.

"Roy, please! Roy, come back to me, I love you! I love you, baby, just stay with me. I need you," she said over and over again for hours. She laid on his lifeless body crying that lonely cry. I wanted to say something to her, but I didn't have the strength to open my mouth. I'd never felt like this before.

The guilt I now held was unbearable. I killed my best friend, and now as I stand over his corpse, I felt even more like a monster. I allowed this woman to get between us, and now that I took him away from her, I don't even have enough courage to say something to her. I reached my hand out to touch her, but my arm froze.

It was like I lost control of my own body. It just wasn't meant to be. I just walked away.

Alone.

Down the path my father placed before me. I thought I was Walker, but now I am a monster. Forever.

⊃⊂⊂

"I don't think I like that story, Todd," Peter said, rubbing his shiny, tired eyes.

"You weren't supposed to like it, young one. Not all the stories are going to be the way you hope. It's just like life. Not everything is going to be the way we think. Life is very unfair and very unforgiving," I replied.

"I hope I never lose my best friend..."

Before he was able to finish his sentence, he stretched his little brown arms, yawned, and closed his eyes.

"Good night."

"Goodnight Todd."

THE END

MR. CLARK DILLON JR

A LOST ART

THE SKY TURNED TO A DARK PURPLE WITH SMALL, BRIGHT STARS filling the blank space. A perfect round and white full moon. To hear all the animals, to feel the gentle cool breeze dance against my face set my spirit at peace. This was truly a beautiful place. Nothing but nature surrounding us. The fireflies lit up the forest, revealing the true green. Too far from any man, at this safe distance man's cold hand couldn't touch us. For this brief second, we were safe from the swift unforgiving touch of man.

Looking into the depth of that oh so dear sky, I still have faith in my brother David. I had no idea when or if we ever were going to reach this perfect place, but when we did, I was going to take full advantage of it once I got there. Embracing it to its fullest, never letting go, and never looking back.

My fatigue was starting to get the best of me so I closed my eyes for a second to sleep. A loud, horrifying scream woke me up. David was being attacked! I could hear him moaning and screaming as my senses started to come back to me. The attacker was something I'd never seen before; it took the form of a wolf or fox. But it was a shade of white that was almost transparent. Its snow fur waved like the waves on a gentle ocean.

I rose up and stared at the creature once; the bright wolf turned and looked at me. It stared at me with pitch blue eyes. It was structured and stood like a lion. My brother's blood dripped off its face ever so lightly.

"Ahh! Oh dear God! Help! Samuel help! Brother! Do something for Christ sake!" David screamed over and over again. The sound of his voice terrified my soul.

The frosty beast growled angrily as it mauled my best friend. With all the strength I had, I charged at it and rammed (pushed) it off of David. The beast weighed a ton, but it fell off and rolled over to where it was back on its feet. I looked at David, and his face and body were covered in blood. Claw marks and gashes opened his flesh. He laid there in the grass barely breathing as he choked to death on his own blood.

The giant winter-like fox stood on all fours staring at me. It growled through its teeth.

I stepped over David and stood my ground in front of my brother. I was too afraid to do anything else; I was sweating with fear, and I knew it could tell that I was scared.

It started walking towards me slowly. One foot at time.

I looked around for a stick or rock that I could use for a weapon. There was nothing around, and he was getting closer.

David grabbed my leg, and I looked down at him. With his lips and no voice, he said, "Run."

In that same instant, the white fox lunged at me. I dove out the way. He flew right over me, and I used that split second to start running away. Leaving David behind took everything out of me. Although I left him without hesitation, I was more afraid of leaving him than I was of the monster.

As I sprinted away, I tried not to look back. I didn't feel anything behind me, but I wasn't thinking that I got rid of the animal. I may have lost the ferocious fox for now, but I lost my brother forever.

Dodging tress, jumping over branches, and crashing through bushes, I did everything I could to get away from the white creature. I ran until I was out of breath, until I couldn't run anymore. This entire forest looked the same, so I couldn't tell where I was. I looked all around and didn't see any sign of that pale beast.

I sat down trying to catch my breath, but I continued to search for the creature. Panting repeatedly, I kept thinking, *What was that thing, and why did it attack us?*

MR. CLARK DILLON JR

"Thought you got rid of me, did you?" A deep voice came from behind.

I shot up in fear and turned around. The snowy monster rested directly behind me. I had no clue it was there; I didn't even hear it approach. I was extremely confused because there was no one else here, but I heard someone speak.

The fox-like animal didn't get up or move; it just laid there and watched me. Still panting, covered in sweat, and scared out my mind, I stood there trying to piece something together, to force this to make sense.

"You look like you've seen ghost, Samuel."

The heavy dark voice came from the creature. Its mouth moved, and words came out. That white demon spoke to me! This didn't make sense. I thought I was dreaming or hallucinating.

"How are you talking? How are you talking?!" I asked again and again until it stood up and I screamed, "What the hell are you?!"

It hopped towards me and smacked me with its paw as it growled with vicious intent.

"Man is forbidden in the forest!" it yelled with fire in its voice.

I fell onto the ground, and the inside of my mouth started bleeding. It felt like I got hit by a train. I spit out some blood and a couple teeth. My head was ringing intensely, and that matched the force my heart was pounding with against my chest.

Watching me with both eyes it, paced back and forth slowly. I rolled over to my stomach and tried to crawl away. I darted forward, and it slammed its leg on my back as it dug its claws deeper into my back. I moaned louder and louder.

"Stop please! Please. I'll leave!" I cried out.

It growled again and then bit me on my side. As I screamed out to God, its many sharp teeth punctured my flesh. It felt like a thousand knives stabbing me all at once. He flipped me over to face him, and it was nothing but anger in his face. No mercy. No forgiveness. I knew he was going to kill me. It stood in the moonlight with my blood dripping from its mouth.

As my last tears rolled down the sides of my face, I continued to whisper, "Please don't kill me. I'm sorry. I'm so, so sorry."

It used its claws to latch on to my shirt and pull my face towards its own. And with a white, bloody face and a murderous grin, it said, "Do not be afraid of those who kill the body but cannot kill the soul. Rather, be afraid of the one who can destroy both soul and body in hell."

I became even more confused because those words soothed me somewhat. More questions started to raise about this creature. I was still very afraid of this animal because it was going to kill me.

"What are you?" I asked with my mouth filling up and overflowing with blood.

It snared then bit my throat and tore out of my neck.

THE END

MR. CLARK DILLON JR

THE CRIMSON TRUTH

WE'VE BEEN LIKE THIS FOR HOURS. The tension in the lobby was steadily raising. We all sweated in fear because we had no clue what their intensions were after they got what they wanted. We didn't know why they were here because this was a charity event. Why would anyone want to steal from this event? This charity event was to raise money for those suffering from breast cancer. Only the worst kind of monsters would try to steal from an event like this.

If I recall correctly, there were about a dozen of us still there. They stormed in shouting and yelling from the top of their lungs, shooting in the air, and throwing people onto the floor. They started grouping us all up together and tying everyone up. We all were blindfolded as well. There was so many of them. They were slapping elder women and screaming at us like animals. This event was dedicated to helping others. These masked men came in causing chaos and terrorizing these noble people. I never thought something like this could ever happen, especially to me. Here, we don't have terrorist attacks; we don't experience disasters, or go through major changes. All of this took me by surprise.

I couldn't see anything; my hands were tied behind my back, and I was kneeling down with another group of hostages. With everything being black, all I could do was listen to those people scream and threaten other hostages. I was shaking in fear, and all I could think about was my daughter and husband. I missed them so much, and I didn't want to die.

But right now, all I had was the people tried up around me. Shaking and crying just like me. We all kneeled close, feeding off each other's strengths or whatever we had left. There was no way any of us were getting through this alone. Although I didn't know these people with me, we stayed close, hoping that we all made it through this together. I could hear a person or two down from me praying softly under their breath, trying not to gain any attention. The sound of teeth chattering and runny noses surrounded me. We all were so scared and didn't know what to do, since we couldn't hug each other we all stayed shoulder to shoulder.

Just having someone next to me helped. It made me feel somewhat safer, like we could get through this if we stayed together.

I could feel them walking back and forth, frustrated. This attack kind of felt unplanned. Almost like it was being dragged out. It was almost easy to tell that they were making things up as they went along. Even when they first came in, it all felt so rushed. I mean, I didn't even hear them ask for the money. They didn't steal anything. This didn't make any sense at all. They were just in here screaming and beating people. I kept waiting for them to ask for the money or for everybody's wallets, but it never happened.

It got quiet for minute or two. Just the sound of heavy breathing and panting filled the air. Then the sound of roaring police sirens came approaching. The police cars drove up on the curb and sidewalk of the building, I could hear the screeching of the tires as they came to an abrupt stop, the car doors opening and slamming shut as the police made their way toward the building. I started to feel more re-lived. I needed them to hurry up and stop these madmen because every second, I became more and more afraid.

"What are we going to do now? They wasn't supposed to arrive this early. None of this is going according to plan," one of them said through their teeth. Even though he was speaking very low, not trying to allow anyone else to hear, I was kneeling so close I was able to listen in.

"You should let us go and turn yourselves in while there is still time!" A manly voice said from someone close to me. There was dead pause for a second, then the sound of gun fire scared us all. The body fell to the ground and heat from the gun warmed me. It sounded like thunder as it echoed throughout the building. I bit my lip trying not to scream, and I cried every tear I had left. All I wanted was my husband. I wanted to go home. I couldn't take this anymore. This was too much for me. I was beginning to lose my mind. The fear had completely taken control of my body.

"Does anyone else have any ideas on we should do?!" the killer loudly asked.

Just the sound of snuffles and crying replied.

I began to pray in my mind. I was out of options, and I was too scared to do anything else. *Please God, help me, oh God deliver me out of the hands of evil. Please, oh my God! I just want to go home. Allow me to make it home safely.*

"We have the building surrounded!"

I wasn't able to make out the rest of what he was saying. A cop was speaking to these monsters from outside. It sounded like God was answering my prayers. I could hear more and more police walk closer to building.

"This isn't part of the plan. We're stuck here. I say let's take a few hostages and bale. He not paying us enough to deal with this."

"No. It won't work. He'll find us if we try to run. We're dead either way, so we might as well do what we came here to do... (long pause) Let's finish what we started."

There wasn't any more talking after that, but I felt them walk past me towards the center of the room.

"Everyone, listen up! I know you all are thinking what are we doing attacking a charity event! Well, we work for a crime lord called Crimson. Crimson wants you all to know that no one is safe. Not even in America. That anything could happen to anyone at any time. You people take everything for granted and appreciate nothing! None of you know what it's like to suffer. Crimson is going change the way you think. To change the way of life. Crimson is simply out to prove just that!"

Immediately after he finished talking, they all opened fire and started shooting the hostages. Bodies fell to the floor soaked in blood carrying multiple bullets. I screamed from the top of my lungs, and *BOOM!* Everyone flew back from an explosion. The sound of glass scattered everywhere.

The police rushed in and started shooting at the murders. I was picked up and dragged during the shootout. As I was being dragged by my hair across all the glass on the floor, cutting my legs. He held the gun over my head, shooting. The sound of screams and gunshots only made me more afraid as it blocked out all other sounds.

"Shut up bitch!" He yelled to me as he stood me up and tightly wrapped his arm around my neck. With my back on him facing the open, the gunfire stopped.

"Follow us, and they die!" someone else yelled. Then I was yanked out the back of the building. I couldn't see anything, but I felt the sun warm my skin. He continued to violently pull and drag me according to his will.

"Freeze!" a voice yelled from a far. More shots were fired from these mad monsters. I screamed again and again, getting louder every time. Bullets ripped past me, ricocheted off the walls and objects around me. Men moaning as they were shot and falling quickly towards the ground. I could tell we were in an alley from the way everything sounded around me. The gun shots continued to fire back and forth. Thunder and fire destroyed everything in their path. The man holding me began screaming and shooting in all directions. He was falling and pulling me down with him. He was no longer using me as a shield but using me as support to stand up. He was struggling extremely hard to stand, then another loud shot came echoing down the alley to hit him.

"Ahhhhha! No!" This scream was more loudly pitched. Sounding more like a woman. He let me go and fell down onto my side. I heard several people running towards me. I was too scared to move or do anything. My heart couldn't take it anymore, so I gave up. I just layed there, accepting whatever happened next.

Someone pulled me off the floor and untied me. Removing the blindfold, I was able to see all the police around me. The relief my soul felt was indescribable. They were asking so many questions, and they surrounded me and walked me out the alley. I looked back, and there were serval men laid out on the ground covered in blood. I had to quickly turn my head back because it was too much to look at.

The street was all blocked off, and there were police cars on each side of the street, creating a barricade. I was walked to an ambulance where I was checked and treated with gentle care. I couldn't be happier or more relived that this was all over. I stared at the ground, keeping my head down while everything went on. I just couldn't wait for this to be over, so that I could go home and see my family.

MR. CLARK DILLON JR

I started to hear more screaming. I looked up and the police were running away from the building waving their arms telling everyone to get out the way. Before anyone else moved or followed their instructions, a white flash blinded us, followed by an explosion. The building exploded, killing everyone inside and everyone around.

Everything went silent, then black forever.

THE END

UNDER THE CALM MOON LIGHT

CHAPTER 1

"How much longer do we have before they reach the city walls?" he asked, staring out into the night.

"Only a matter of minutes, my Lord," I replied. I could see the fear and pain in his eyes. He didn't say anything else or give any other commands. He just continued to stare out into the darkness outside.

"My Lord, I think it's time to prepare the men," I suggested.

"I need you to go and protect my people. Because of my doings, a terrible tragedy will fall upon the people. You must do everything you can to protect them. Do you understand?"

"I do."

"I'm sorry, my friend. You don't deserve this, and neither do the people. You were like a son to me. (Pause) Don't come back for me. Make sure my family is safe, and get them out of the city."

"I understand, my King," I answered back.

He turned and leaned in with his arms stretched out lightly. After he hugged me, he went back to looking outside. I then darted down the steps and into the throne room, where the council members, captains, and royal family awaited.

"Sound the alarms and get all men ready to defend their home. You two, take each a dozen men and guard the tunnels underground" (the two captains replied right away and left to perform their task). "I want women and children removed from their homes and taken to the tunnels. It's dark out, so take the torches and lanterns to light your way. Leave no one behind. We must move swiftly because we are out of time..."

Before I could finish talking the queen stepped forward and asked, "Are these my husband's orders? Are we to leave at once?" Sorrow filled my voice, but I was not going to sit here and explain everything to her.

"Yes, they are. You and daughter need to come with me right away. Everyone else, go and gather the rest of the men and form a perimeter around the kingdom. May the Gods favor us tonight!" I stated. I walked over to the queen and grabbed her hand. She and her daughter followed me as I led them out the back, outside, to where my personal regiment waited for me. I needed them out of the way and safe, so I could focus on the townspeople.

"I want you all to protect the royal family. They go nowhere unless all of you accompany them. You die first, their lives are the priority! Is that clear?!" I ordered.

"Yes sir!" they all answered together.

I approached Sir Peter (my second in command) to a have private word with him.

"I need you to get them out of the city any way you can. Don't stop for anything or help anyone else. I'll come find you once I'm done here in the city. Peter, I'm asking you to do this as my friend, not my solider. I need you one this one," I begged quietly.

"Don't worry about them. Do what you need to do. I will see to it with my life that they make it out of the city unharmed. You have my word," he responded, smiling. He embraced me with a hug then went to carry out my command.

I turned around to head back inside, but I was stopped.

"Are you not going to see to our safety? Where are you going?" the queen asked as she picked up her little Elizabeth and held her close. Step by step, she got a little closer to me.

"Unfortunately, I do not have time to explain this to you. You need to trust me and do as I say. I will come back for you. I swear."

She understood me. A few tears rolled down her face.

MR. CLARK DILLON JR

"Come back. Please. I need you."

I nodded my head, telling her that I would. I wished I could go with them and make sure they made it out myself. This was the first time I had to leave her behind like this. It didn't feel right. I'd never seen the queen like this before. So full of fear. I had to go on.

I continued on inside and ran to the front, where the men were gathering all women and children and leading them into the tunnels to escape. Torches hung in the air and lit pathways through the houses and sheds, Women struggled to carry their personal items and children at the same time, manifolds of people everywhere doing multiple/different things at same time caused chaos. Babies crying; people rushing. It was so much going on.

I looked up. The full white moon made everything seem so calm. It was just bright enough to reveal the faint clouds drifting above. I started helping people along, helping them get to the tunnels before the enemy arrived.

Above all the chaos, I heard a man yell, "Incoming!"

I immediately looked up and saw a fire ball arching over the city walls. Everyone stopped and stared at the fire as someone screamed, "Oh! My! God!!" The fire ball exploded onto the shed, throwing fire everywhere. The screams grew louder, and people became uncontrollable. I did everything I could to keep them going into the tunnels. Soldiers attempted to put out the fire. But nothing seemed to be working.

"Incoming!" was once more yelled, and more fire balls flew over and smashed into the city. I was doing all I could, trying to keep a calm head. I saw the men running towards the gates, the city entrance, so followed to the best of my ability. There were so many people, it was hard getting past everyone. The gates exploded into pieces, knocking everyone around onto the ground.

Out of the noise and debris, an army marched in. There were thousands of them. Tens of thousands, it seemed like. And out of the darkness and into the city they came wearing dark silver armor, and each of them had a red cross insignia on their helmets. They drew their weapons, and with a war cry from hell, they began the slaughter. One by one, they killed soldiers, women, and children, plunging their blades through my men's chests and chopping their heads off.

Seeing my people, my friends, die right in front of me did something to me. It triggered something within me. Limbs cut off, women tossed around, and my brothers in arms fighting to their last breath. Blood shot in the air, silencing the screams. The smell disturbed my soul.

"No!" I yelled as I charged at the enemy. I drew my blade and rammed it into the enemy's chest. Kicking him off onto the ground captured the attention of a few more, so as they ran at me, one would swing his sword, but I would step to the side, dodging his attack, giving me time and space to swing my sword up and cut his throat open. With his blood spilling out on the ground, the next solider swung, and I parried his attack. I kicked him in the side of his knee, dropping him, and swinging down to decapitate him.

After catching my breath, another came at me, but he was no different. After making enough space, I chopped his arm off and punched him in the side of his head. I found myself surrounded. I held my sword out, pointing it at them, yelling, "What are you afraid of?"

One, two at a time—it didn't matter. I would dodge as much as I could, and if I couldn't, I parried every other attack. I was fast enough to where if I saw an opening, it was a kill. I chopped off arms, legs, heads... I must have killed six people, and I wanted more. Covered in blood, the smell didn't bother me. I grabbed one by his arm and snapped it out of place. As he screamed with true pain, I struck my blade through his forehead. Pulling the sword out, I split his head in half.

I was breathing heavy, but I didn't feel tired or weak. I held my sword up, and they continued to pour in. I completely forgot what I was fighting for; I lost all control, and I didn't care. The bodies kept coming, and I kept sending them to their graves. I had gotten lost in the war. I punched one in the face, kicked him in the balls, and when he dropped his head, I stuck my sword through his neck. Another grabbed me by my waist and threw me onto the ground, causing me to drop my sword. I grabbed a blade from a fallen solider and drove it into his side. I head-butted him, tossing him to the side. I found myself surrounded again, but this time, no one attacked.

I kept looking around at all of them, waiting for one them to strike. Behind them I saw the rest of those monsters, finishing off the rest of my people. One

MR. CLARK DILLON JR

man stepped forward. His armor was different from the others. He was taller, and his armor was all black. He drew his sword and spoke, "Fight me warrior. For you are worthy." (Even his sword was black.)

He took another sword and handed it to me. I wasn't impressed, not by him or his fancy sword. I was going to kill him and then I was going to kill everybody else. I took the weapon.

The circle that surrounded me backed up, providing us with a lot more space. The dark knight attacked me, but I stayed one step ahead of him. He swung again and again but could never land a blow. He swung, but I dropped below the blade and cut him on his leg.

As he dropped on the wounded leg, I punched him across the face. He slowly turned his face back to show that my punch didn't hurt him. So I punched him over and over and over again until his helmet flung into the air and landed behind him. I went to punch him again, but he caught my fist and twisted my arm. As I moaned and dropped, he stood up and kneed me in the stomach. He threw me into the surrounding men.

I tried to get up as fast as I could, but the man approached me too fast and swung his sword at my body. I jumped out of the way, but he still cut my left side. He went to swing again, to finish me off, but I picked up my sword and blocked his attack. With our blades caught together, he began to push me back down to the ground. He was clearly stronger than me, so I dropped my sword, moved out the way, making him slam his sword into the ground.

Before mine dropped to floor, I caught it with my other hand, spun, and swung it over into his back and out his chest, killing him instantly. Even through their helmets, I could see faces. They were more than surprised. They couldn't believe that I killed him. I pulled the sword back out and stood ready for the next attacker.

The circle that surrounded opened up, and a horseman made its way to me.

The man on the horse looked down on me and said, "What's your name, knight?"

I kept my guard up, but none of them had their weapons out. They made it seem like we were no longer fighting.

"Abel. Son of Matthew," I answered, still breathing heavily.

He kept looking at me, then he spoke again.

"Take him! He's coming with us. Kill everyone else!"

Everything went black after that. Silencing the world.

CHAPTER 2

THE DEVIL'S GRIP

I FELT SICK TO MY STOMACH. Every part of my body ached. For weeks, I'd been in bondage. The nights were freezing, and the days were long and dry. I smelt like piss and dirt, and I'd barely eaten anything. This whole time we'd been traveling, but I had no idea where we were going.

I was packed in the back of this wagon, which carried their wounded soldiers. Most of the wounded died a few days ago. They just were not strong enough to survive this journey. We'd traveled through the woods and up the mountains, and I couldn't tell where we were. I felt like I was going to die as well if we did not reach our destination soon. I can still hear the cries from my people who were all slain right in front of me. All those innocent women and children, murdered. Life can be so cruel, but I had no idea it could reach this level. Even the young ones were showed no mercy as they stabbed, stomped, and beat them to bloody death. Good men that fought by my side for their families were torn into pierces and never got a proper burial. I didn't even want to remember what they did to the women.

During this time, I kept thinking about my King, and how he made it my responsibility to protect the people. His people. What did he do to bring this on? What could he have possibly done to bring such tragedy upon so many people? I keow he just stood there in his tower, watching from above. Watching his men get destroyed, his children killed, and his women raped before they were executed. I felt so much anger, and there was nothing I could do about it. I looked at that man as my father. I respected that man more than I had anyone else. He let me down, and I could never forgive him for that. I wonder if the queen and her daughter made it out? I'm sure he watched them as well.

The wagon stopped. Footsteps came to my side. The man grabbed me and elbowed me across the face, turning everything black once more.

As I started to gain consciousness, I knew that two men were dragging me by my arms. They dropped me onto the ground; I raised my head. I was in a throne room before a king. Armed guards were all along the walls leading to a chair made of solid gold in the middle of the room. The king sat and starred at me from his golden throne.

"Tell me, young man, why have you been brought before me?" the king asked with a firm and deep voice. I tried to stand up, but I only had the energy to kneel. I didn't answer his question. "I'm not going to ask again boy, so you better answer," he said, but this time with anger in his tone.

With the energy I had, I said, "Why did you kill my people?"

He chuckled and then stood up. As he walked over to me, his long red cape softly hovered over the floor. His tall stature with long white hair only made him look more intimidating. Once he approached me, he crouched to my eye level. His crown was pure gold with strange engravings on it. It was a pattern; the pattern looked like water. I looked him in his eyes, but he had no pupils, his eyes were just white. White like milk.

"Your people? You were just a knight, they were not your people," he said slowly.

"Those people you killed were mine. And they did nothing wrong. I am going to make sure you pay for what you have done," I replied.

"You have such a hot fire that burns within you. I like that. I think you are going to like it here." He stood up and started walking back to his chair. "Once I see what you can do, I will then decide how you spend the reminder of your time here."

"If you think I'm..."

Before I could finish talking, he gently raised his hand, and I felt a force come over me and squeeze my insides. Everything felt so hot; I dropped to the floor and curled up, and my insides felt like they were being crushed. I moaned and screamed out, but no one did anything. The guards just watched. Through all my pain, I heard the King speak again.

"You will do as you're told! And obey my every command. You belong to me now, boy. You best start acting like it."

He lowered his hand and sat down. That powerful force left me, and the pain subsided. The two guards picked me back up and dragged me out the throne room.

I awoke some time later in a cell. I got up and walked toward the bars. There were cells all long the hall, and each cell was holding someone. It was dark, only a few lanterns lit this entire place/hall.

"Oh wow look at you," A voice said from behind. I turned around, and there was an old man sitting up against the wall on the floor.

"What is this place? Why am I here?" I asked, desperately looking for answers.

"You have been chosen to fight. I'm not worried about you, young man. You seem like you can handle yourself."

"I don't understand. Fight for what? Why are we fighting?" I asked, walking closer to him.

"You met the King, yes? He's sees something in you. I think I see it too. What-ever you do, don't let him down," the old man said.

I sat down next to him. The old man closed his eyes and gently fell asleep. His chest slowly rising and lowering as he breathed. I watched him for a few; he was at peace. I closed my eyes as well and joined him in sleep.

"On your feet! On your feet, boy!" a voice shouted. I awoke and saw a man yelling at me. I looked over and the old man was missing. I stood up, and the guard came into my cell to grab me. He then started dragging me down the hall. I kept looking into the different cells as we passed. Men who all looked lost; men who looked mentally defeated. Most of them were covered in scars and dry blood. I still did not see the old man who I spoke with yesterday. I was taken into a dirty room where I was given light armor, food, and water. I ate as much as I could before the food was taken away. Then I was dragged into another room filled with weapons.

"Choose a weapon, and choose wisely," the guard commanded. I grabbed a sword and passed up on the spear and shield. The guard smiled a little bit and guided me through another room and into a dark tunnel. I saw an opening at the end and the tunnel and heard faint cheering from many people. "Head towards the end of the tunnel. And good luck," he said.

I started walking slowly, and as I got closer to the end, the cheering and screaming from the people became louder and louder. Once I got to the end and walked out, I was in a giant stadium (arena). The first thing that hit me was the light; it was like the sun was starring directly down upon me. The sky was a beautiful bright blue without a cloud in sight. It was like nothing I'd ever seen before.

Thousands of people (above) surrounded me. They were screaming and chanting; it looked like complete chaos. Women and children were in the stands as well. The walls around me had to be hundreds of feet high. Watching all the people look down on me made me feel like I was some kind of animal in a pit. A dark figure made its way out of the tunnel that was across from me on the other side of the pit. It was a man; his pants were torn and covered in old blood. Wearing no shirt, his body was dripping in mud, but he did have on a helmet. His helmet was in the shape of a raven. Carrying his spear and shield, he started making his way towards me. I knew I had no choice but to face this warrior in combat, so I began to make my way towards him. As we got closer, we continued to pick up speed until we were fully sprinting at each other.

"Ahhhh!" I yelled as I jumped and swung my sword at his head. The fighter blocked my attack with his shield. I stepped back and waited for him to strike, which he did. He lunged spear first, but I side stepped and parried his strike. I ran forward and punched him in the stomach. Swinging his shield over his head, he bashed me in the head. As I stumbled back, he kicked me onto the ground. Then he leaped up, coming down spear first, but I rolled backwards, out of the way. His spear slammed into the ground.

I jumped up; I kicked his elbow in and grabbed his arm as it leaned in then I flipped him onto the ground. Swinging my sword over with the death blow, he moved his spear to counter my swing just in enough time. He started to moan as I pressed my sword down harder on his spear. I could feel him weakening. He head-butted me to clear some space, so he could stand up. He threw his shield.

I slid under it, but as I stood up, he lunged in (forward towards me) with the spear, but I spent (around the spear) causing him to completely miss me with that attack. Because I stepped forward when I spent, it put me right within range to kill him. I stabbed him right in the stomach. He spit blood all over my hands and sword. He dropped his spear, and before his body dropped to the ground, I caught him by his neck and started punching him over and over in the mouth and face. Then I pulled the sword out of his stomach, chopped his head off, and kicked him onto the ground.

As his burning red blood leaked out his neck, the crowd went crazy and screamed louder. As I gazed over the crowd, I saw the king I had met. He was watching as well. This is what the old man must have been talking about. Two more figures made their way out of the tunnel. They were both women, and they didn't have any weapons or armor. Both of them wore torn dirty black dresses, their skin was gray, and long, unkempt hair covered their faces. One's fingernails were long and black. I did not care what they looked like I was not going to fight unarmed women. I lowered my sword and my guard to show them I wasn't a threat. I walked a little closer to them and yelled, "I'm not going to fight you two!"

The crowd went completely silent. It was almost scary how quiet it got. No one said or did anything. The people just stared at me. My body felt frozen; I was so nervous. I didn't want to move. The women never moved another muscle after exiting the tunnel.

"Sister! Give me strength!" One of the women yelled with her hands stretched out towards the sky. Thick gray clouds formed quickly then lighting struck her hands. She then pointed her hands at me, and lighting flew towards me, but I rolled out of the way and just like that the crowd began screaming and cheering again. The other girl ran at me with speeds I didn't know were possible. I couldn't tell which direction she was coming; she jumped on me and sank her dagger-like teeth into my shoulder. I cried out and then slammed her onto the ground. Another lighting blot jolted towards me, but I saw it coming and jumped out the way. It hit the ground and dirt exploded into the air.

The girl I slammed darted out of the dirt and punched my sword out of my hand, then punched me four times in the chest and stomach. She was swinging for another punch, but I caught her fist and twisted it. Then I grabbed the back of

MR. CLARK DILLON JR

her head and kneed her in the face twice before elbowing her in the neck. She screeched out loud like a cat, jumped onto my shoulders, and then flipped me on the floor with her feet. I saw another bolt of lightning heading my way, so grabbed the girl and kicked her into the lighting. The girl screamed a miserable cry before exploding into black dust. The crowd's cheering only grew louder.

I picked up my sword and charged at the second woman. She hovered toward me, dropped down, and tripped me onto my back. She drove her claws into my side and moaned out in pain. She kept swinging her hands wildly at me, but I blocked her claws as much as I could with my sword. She scratched me a few times through my armor. I was beginning to lose too much blood. She swung with her left hand down, and a whip of lighting followed. She continued to swing and whip lighting at me, but I was fast enough to stay out of range by dodging and moving out of the way.

Her frustration grew as she was not able to hit me. She jumped and slammed both hands on the ground, launching both whips down, but I dropped and rolled backwards out of the way and leaped forward at her. Plunging my sword straight through her face, I pushed down and sliced her completely in half. Her blood soaked me and filled the air.

The crowd went crazy! Everyone stood up and shouted with high praise. I'd never seen so many people happy; I also had never seen women control the power of lighting. Everything I knew was changing. This world was no longer the way I remembered. But if I had to fight in the arena, I was going to give it my all to survive because I was not going to die here. I made a promise that I had to keep.

TO BE CONTINUED...

Under the Calm Moon Light
will return in Volume Two

INTO THE DARK

PART ONE

"One more story, Todd. Please?" the little voice asked with excitement. He held his little brown hands out and reached for me. I lowered my head and allowed him to rub his soft, fragile fingers through my fur.

"Peter, what is it that you believe in? What scares you the most?" (His glossy big eyes widened.) "Nothing really scares me anymore. But there is someone who keeps me awake at night. His only purpose is to ruin and to destroy you. The one soul that cannot be redeemed."

"Are you talking about the Devil? H-have you ever seen him?" the curious voice asked.

"Yes. But this is a story about someone else. Someone who found him," I replied.

∞

"FIVE DAYS IN THIS GOD FORSAKEN JUNGLE!" I exclaimed, wiping the sweat off my forehead. The sun still found its way through the trees as it blinded our path in front. Surrounded by nothing but trees and the sound of heavy breathing from us, colorful birds screeched in the trees high above us. Ugly, dark moneys swung from the branches. Annoying bugs and insects buzzed all around us. I could still hear the river from nearby which flowed ever so softly. I grabbed the canteen dangling from my waist for one more small drink of water. I raised it above it my face and shook the last drops of water out. When nothing but a few drops fell and evaporated on my tongue, I leaned against a tree and put my head down, sighing with deep disappointment.

"You drank all of that too fast, my friend. I told you to drink it wisely. We have a long trip ahead of us," he spoke as he carefully walked past me. I watched him walk on by as if I didn't hear what he just said. I looked at the others, and they were dying, just as I was. We were not hikers or mountain climbers—we were scientists. I'd spent most of my life with my head in a book. I was not even a jogger, for Christ sake. The five of us set out on the expedition to prove something to ourselves. Yes, we wanted to prove to everyone that this flower was out there and that it could heal and help people like we knew it could. But we wanted to do this for ourselves. Show ourselves that we were not afraid to get our hands dirty. That we just didn't belong in some lab.

"Alright, can we please take a break? My feet are killing me," Alice pleaded as she stopped in her tracks and placed her hands on her hips, hanging her head down. Samuel paused (turned around) and looked at the exhaustion in all our faces.

"Okay, sure, let's take a break. But we need to be up and moving soon if you want to reach your destination before sundown," Samuel replied.

We all removed our bags and sat down for a second. It was so unbelievably hot, and my feet were killing me, so I was glad Alice spoke up because I really needed a second to rest. But no matter how hot or tired, I was not going to give up. I could not give up now; we had come too far. I looked at William, and he kept slapping himself in the face because of the bugs. He didn't want to come down here. Him more than anyone, and I don't blame him now. This had been the worst week of my life. But back in the States, it seemed like such a good idea. Plus, we needed to do this for people around the world, like William's father. William's father suffered from lung cancer then eventually lost his life two years ago. More people died from lung cancer than any other disease in the world. The Magin flower had the properties to fight lung cancer like no other drug will. Think about how many lives we could save if there was actually some type of drug that could fight the cancer in human lungs. The Magin flower might not be able to cure lung cancer for good, but it could give people like William's father a real fighting chance to survive.

Joey slowly stood up and walked behind a tree. You could hear his zipper unzip, as he exhaled and released. It was rather disturbing because he was so close, listening to him moan in relief as he shakes himself dry. Michelle mumbled (to herself), "Have some professionalism, please."

Samuel gave us all that look, and it was time to get moving again. As Samuel led the way, we realized we may have bitten off more than what we could chew by coming to this island. We had never been so tired and so scared in our entire lives. The only thing pleasant about this trip was the boat ride over here to the island, and Sam's boat was dirty. Plus, it smelled. We figured we would have our work cut out for us when we all agreed to come on this trip. We just weren't expecting it to be this extreme. Well, I wasn't expecting it to be this hard. Michelle and I were the ones who started this whole thing. It was our idea to set out and find the flower, and we were responsible for this mission, considering the fact we are the lead scientists for the Magin flower and this expedition. William and Joey are next up. They helped us with researching the Magin and its healing properties. They also created a container, which is a way to preserve the flower on the trip back to the States. Alice helped Michelle and I locate the flower. We all found where it grows, and we needed it in order to recreate its environment and then eventually mass produced.

∞G

(BACK IN THE UNITED STATES;
FOUR DAYS EARLIER)

I felt my phone vibrating in my pocket. As I tried to stay on road, I reached down and grabbed my phone recklessly. Just before I thought it was going to voicemail, I answered, "Hello this Dillon."

"Dillon, where are you?" (Spoken in a light, cute voice.)

"Sorry, I'm running just a few minutes late. I'll be there in like three minutes or so."

"That's fine just wanted to make sure you were at least on your way (chuckling). Also I talked to Alice and William; they're going to meet us at the hanger," she said with a smile in her voice.

"Okay, great. I spoke with Joey yesterday. He should be meeting us there as well."

"(Sigh) Does he really have to come? I feel like this trip will be easier and better without him." I could hear the disappointment in her tone.

"Yes, Michelle. He's just as much a part of this as everyone else." She had never really liked Joey. To be honest, no one did. He was a cool guy and very intelligent, but there was a huge downfall or flaw in his personality. He was a dick. Since we started the Magin project, all five of us had been working closely over the past years and really gotten to know each other rather well. A true bond was formed, and we turned into really close friends. One thing that we all could agree on is that Joey is a tool. At times, it became almost impossible to work with him, which has disappointing because we really needed his help. I didn't really care for his antics at all.

I pulled up to her house and honked the horn. It was raining just a little bit, and the sky was completely gray. I watched the windshield wipers go back and forth for a minute or two and then she came outside with like four bags. She was really struggling trying to get to the car, so I got out and said, "We're not going on vacation."

As I grabbed a few of her bags, I put them in the backseat because she was going to fill the trunk completely. She jumped in the passenger seat trying to shield her hair from the rain with her hands.

"I'm not sure where we are going to put all your clothes once we get on the plane." I said jokingly, laughing a little.

"I know you'll figure something out. You're smart," she said back with a fake smile. On our way to the airport hangar, we went over some last minute calculations and plans. She pulled out the map of the island.

"Okay Dillon. What if the flower isn't there? I mean all our research puts the Magin flower in the middle of that island, but it's still only an 81 percent chance that it is there."

I could feel her looking at me, and I felt the worry too.

"Well, it's a little late to be thinking the flower isn't going to be there, but don't worry the flower is going to be there. All of our research has brought us to that area on the island. We've been planning and searching for years about the Magin flower. Have a little faith!" I tried to sound encouraging for her, but I don't think it was working.

"Dillon, we have to tell the others that there is a chance that the flower might not be there. That isn't fair."

"No, Michelle. As far as they are concerned, the flower is there."

For the next 22 minutes, it was a quiet, somewhat awkward car ride. I wanted to say something. Not how I felt about her, but I just wanted to break the silence. We arrived at the (private) hangar, and I saw William and Alice's car parked off to the side. As a silent team, Michelle and I grabbed all the bags and started making our way onto the plane. Since this plane was rented by all of us, it was a pretty decent size plane. No first-class accommodations by any means, but enough space for everyone and Michelle's bags.

When I got on the plane, William approached me, gave me a light hug, and said, "It's about time you two made it. Oh, by the way, this is the pilot. You three haven't been properly introduced yet."

I turned around and a young man greeted Michelle and I.

Shaking his hand, I said, "Thank you for doing this. This means a lot to us and the world."

"Don't sweat it. You all let me know when you're ready for takeoff, and we'll be on our way," the pilot replied. He then walked back to the cockpit, and Alice told me "good morning" but then started talking to Michelle. I could tell Alice was really scared about going on this trip just by her over all body language. But we all were.

William sat down and pointed out the window.

"Here come yo boy," he said laughing.

Instantly the girls turned around and saw Joey walking up towards the plane. Looking at Michelle, it was almost like I could read her mind. I knew she hated Joey, and her look said it all when he came in.

"Well, with all the money we put in, I thought we'd be flying in Air Force One!" Joey said, laughing as he looked around in disappointment.

"Good morning to you, too, sir," William said as he got up to shake his hand.

We all talked for a second and went over the game plan one more time before we told the pilot we were ready for takeoff. I explained to everyone that we were not doing this for money or to become famous, but that we are doing this to help others. To give others a fighting chance, a real fighting chance to survive. When I was talking, everyone kept taking turns looking at Will (I did my best to not look at him), but I'm sure he knew we all were looking at him. He tried to be strong, but we all knew what he was thinking about.

Alice got up to let the pilot know it was time. Michelle tapped Joey on the shoulder whispered, "I know you joined this trip so you can have your 15 minutes of fame when we return, but for once, try doing something for someone else and not just yourself."

Joey didn't even say anything back; he just smiled. Alice sat down, the engine started up, and the plane began to move. The plane crept out the hangar, and the propellers picked up speed. Everyone buckled in and gripped the arm rest. I rested my head back and closed my eyes. The plane was in full motion. The plane got higher and higher.

On our way up, I felt my stomach drop. No matter how many times I flew in a plane, the takeoff gets me every time.

"It's gonna be like this for the next 10 hours," Joey said, laughing at everyone. But for the most part, he was right. The plane was more than capable of making this type of flight. So once we reached the appropriate attitude, I got up, walked to the bar, and started pouring myself a drink. I could hear Alice slowly walking

MR. CLARK DILLON JR

toward me, saying, "I really need a drink" under her breath. Alice wasn't a huge fan of flying either. I turned around and handed her a glass.

"Wow, you can hear him snoring from a mile away. We haven't even been flying for that long, and he's already knocked out sleep," she said about Will, taking a sip.

"I don't know how he can sleep through this. But this is how black people deal with flying, they just sleep through it," I replied trying to maintain my balance standing up. She laughed a little, but she tried to ignore the joke. (Which was pretty funny, if I say so myself).

"I never thought I could do something like this. To leave everything behind and go out to try and find something important, something that may not even exist. We will change everything once we find the flower."

Before I was even able to say anything back to Alice, Joey stepped in and spoke his mind, "That's if we find the flower, love. Which we better, because I left a nice lab and study back at home to be going to some sweat infested jungle."

"Oh shut up, Joey! You left because you wanna put your face on the flower and act like some hero when we return!" Michelle chimed with such emotion.

Will started smiling in his sleep. He knew it was only a matter of time before they got into it.

"Like it or not, Joey is part of the team. He helped just as much as the rest of us, so he deserves to be here. We need to start acting like a team and not a bunch of kids!" I yelled.

The plane went completely silent. I took my last sip and sat down. After about a few minutes of silence Will said, "Only nine in half more hours to go," with his eyes still shut and grinning through his teeth.

The next nine hours weren't that bad. Everyone could still tell that Michelle was still a little upset about me speaking out at everyone because she felt like was it was mainly towards her.

Once the plane landed, we all gathered our things and stepped outside. Instantly, you could tell the difference. We arrived in South America. The smell was the first thing that hit you. We were not by any major cities or anything, but much rather towards the shore. We landed in Ecuador, which is right at the edge of

South America. We made sure we had everything and then we took a small bus to the ocean (docking area/beach for boats). The bus was packed with people, and they smelled unbearable. We all were bunched up together real close. Joey was basically sitting in my lap and said (with his hot stinky breath smiling extra hard), "Would a yo mama joke be inappropriate right now?"

"Yes, it would, so shut up," I answered quickly, trying to get him to stop talking.

We had arranged a meeting to meet a man named Samuel Rivero, a native of this land and our guide to take us to the island. Michelle and I talked to him before because he helped an archaeologist that we knew a while back. He helped them get through the South American jungle to find some artifact, which turned out to be nothing once they got back to the United States. So, we made contact with him, and he agreed to take us on his boat the island and be our guide once we got there. We knew that the flower grew somewhat in the middle of the island. But the island was mostly jungle, and we were going to need some help getting through it. Once we got to the ocean (docks) Samuel was waiting by the docks next to his boat. The boat was in rather poor condition and got the group worried. Samuel made his way toward us, but none of us moved because we all were busy staring at his boat.

"Don't you people worry. She'll get you where you need to go. This boat and I have been to hell and back, and she's still in good condition," Samuel said with great confidence smiling extra hard.

"Good condition?" Joey whispered to himself.

"I hope so Samuel, we're all counting on you. This is Alice Jao, Joey Fish, William Harris, and of course you already know Michelle Thompson and myself," I said introducing everyone. One by one, we shook his dirty hand (as he smiled and nodded his head in excitement shaking it back). Afterwards, we then we loaded up onto his boat. The inside was just as bad as the outside. It was really dirty, but at least he took all the junk and pushed it to one side of the boat. It was all small stuff, like empty beer bottles, canned food, and a little trash (so it didn't unbalance the boat). I thought that was rather funny, so I stood there for a second looking at it.

Joey came and stood next to me. After a brief moment he said, "Well at least he shoved all his trash onto one side of the boat for us."

Although it wasn't the nicest boat, it was rather large with more than enough space for all of us. The ride across the open water was more than pleasant. Will and Joey were going over more of the procedure on what to do once they have the flower and how to preserve it for the trip back home. Joey had designated two special containers for the flowers once we found them. He made two containers, and he gave one to me. I went to the table Michelle and Alice were sitting at. They had the maps out and were trying to figure out the best route to get to the center of the island.

"Well, we know the flower is in a cave. From what I know, the cave is in some type of drop off point. Like a big hole in the ground. So you want to be very carefully planning our approach because the ground could be shifted toward that drop off and lead into the hole," I said, pointing at the middle of the map.

"Right. But we don't know when the ground will shift like that," Alice said, still looking at the map. As Alice and Michelle continued to talk about the location and how to find it, I looked up and watched the waves roll on by as we got closer to the island and their voices faded off into the background. The crystal-clear water splashed into the air. The water sparkled like it was filled with floating diamonds. The strong blue waves curled and collided into the boat.

"This island is pretty much all jungle, so dress according please!" Samuel yelled from a far. William came up to us, and once again he expressed his feelings about going into the jungle looking for the flower. Don't get me wrong, everyone was scared but Will was the only one who repeatedly expressed his concern about this expedition.

Samuel yelled once more, "Just a few minutes until we beach."

At that moment, everyone started packing up and getting ready to hit the island. Once we beached, I was the first one to walk on the hot soft sand, and feeling the sun hit my face felt amazing. Not a cloud in sight, and the sky was just as blue as the water. The jungle was alive. Listening to all the animals and birds gave me goosebumps. Everyone grabbed their gear and all that was necessary for the mission.

As Samuel finished tying the boat down, he explained to us that we had one rule: Stick together! No one got left behind. We were ready for this. Although we all were scared out our minds, we couldn't be more excited about finding the Magin flower.

"Alright! Stay close, and stay alert." Samuel said as he led the way into the loud, live jungle. Like trained soldiers, we followed him one by one into the wild green. Trees as tall as skyscrapers, a sight to truly behold. Even in this heat, we all were in awe at this beautiful green wonderland.

For hours on hours, we walked and made our way through the jungle; talking breaks periodically helped, but we were carrying so much gear and doing so much walking, it made it seem impossible. The sun was merciless, and the day stretched on forever. After so long, the sun began to drop. Samuel made it very clear that once it started to get dark, we needed to set up camp and rest until the sun returned. So, we did stop, and Samuel gave everyone simple instructions to make the area we were in as nice as possible for us to sleep. This was going to be the first time I slept in a jungle, and hearing all the sounds wasn't making it easy.

Samuel and William built a small shelter. All of us would have to lay close if we all were going to fit under the roof. As we were getting close to completing everything, William said, "I'm really glad we got through this day and that the sun went down because it was way too hot, and I need to rest for more than five minutes."

"I agree with you whole heartedly, Will! This was a lot for me. I knew it was going to be a lot, but I had no idea it would be like this," Alice agreed.

Samuel shook his head and laughed a little to himself.

"Let me guess chief. This is funny to you? Watching us suffer." Joey said to Samuel.

"I know you people are very smart. I see this. But there is more to life than reading a book," Samuel replied. It was getting pretty dark, but I could still see the straight ugly face that Joey used to stare at Samuel.

"That may be true, but I'm glad we all decided to do this. This shows that Sam is right, and we are willing to go out and see the world just as we are willing to study it," I added.

"I like that answer, Dillon, and you are correct" (Walking toward me). "Although you are a spoiled bunch, I am happy to help and be here on this journey with you," Samuel said, ending by placing his hand on my shoulder.

"We appreciate you, Samuel. Once we get this fire going, maybe it will force away some of these bugs away," Michelle said changing the subject. That was the signal to hurry up and get the fire going.

Since it was my task to supply the fire wood, Samuel stopped what he was doing and helped me get everything going. We dug a hole and placed the wood down. Once the fire was lit, the jungle around us and provided warmth as the sun retired for the day. Everything outside the wall of light from the fire was pitch black. We held our hands out trying to capture the warmth.

Sam stood up and said that he would watch out for this night while we tried to get some sleep. Alice and Michelle laid next to each other with William on the right side of them. I wanted to lay next to Michelle, and I wasn't going to tell William to get up or anything. With Joey lying next to me, I made it my goal to sleep next to Michelle the tomorrow night.

"Hey, Dillon. I can see the disappointment all in your face," Joey said smiling really big.

"What are you talking about now?" I replied.

"You know exactly what I'm talking about. You want to be laying on the other side of William."

"Give it a rest, will you? Leave me alone. I just want to get some sleep," I said, turning my back to him.

I felt his head hover above my shoulder as he said, "Don't worry, friend. I know what you want."

He went back to his side and fell asleep. Even with the jungle being as loud as it was, I still was able to go right to sleep.

"Rise and shine everyone!" A loud voice yelled as it woke me up. As I tried to wake myself up, I rubbed my eyes for a minute. Something smelt rather good. I looked around, and everyone was stretching/yawning and trying to wake them-selves up. Samuel had cooked something using the fire from last night. As he chewed the mystery meat that he cooked, he said, "You all should eat a little some-thing so we can get moving."

"Don't worry guys, I packed food for us. Because I am not eating whatever he is," Alice said standing up. She reached for her bag and pulled out food for everyone. She even offered some to Samuel. She had water, sandwiches, nuts, and fruit. Together as a team, we sat down and ate before we got up to leave. After a few minutes, once everyone was done, it was time to get going again. We all gathered our gear, and Samuel began to lead the way through the jungle. With the girls behind him, William, and Joey behind me, we continued on our way. We walked, and we walked. Hiking up ridges, crossing shallow rivers, and carefully walking down muddy slopes.

"Please be careful! Watch your step because I'm seeing a lot of mud slides," Sam yelled from up front. We had already gone down a couple muddy slopes, but they weren't that steep.

"Woah," William said trying to maintain his balance.

"You alright there, big guy?" Joey asked, laughing a little.

"Yeah, I'm okay. I just stepped in some mud or something," he replied. I turned around; William was smiling, and Joey started to laugh a little louder. As soon as William started to join Joey in the laughter, he dropped to the floor, slammed down, and mud flew up in the air, and he started sliding down.

"Oh God! Samuel help! Will just dropped!" I yelled as William moaned in fear, trying to slow himself down by grabbing onto rocks and tree branches. Samuel came back swiftly to where Will dropped, and without thinking about it (he looked at me then back at the trail that Will left behind as he slide down), he dropped his things and gear and slid down after him.

"This man is a freaking superhero!" Joey said, watching him slide down after William.

"Where's Will? Guys, is everything alright back there?" Michelle asked, trying to walk her way back to us.

"No! No, stay right there. Don't move; it's not safe," I said back, holding my hand up and warning her to stop walking.

"Dillon, we have to find a way to meet back up with them. Samuel is the only one who can get us to the flower," Joey said taking big steps to me.

"Dillon! Dillon! Dillon, can you hear me?" a voice yelled from down the mud slide.

"Yes! Samuel, is that you?" I yelled back down.

"Yes! Drop some rope so we can climb back up!" he loudly responded.

"Alright! One minute!" I said to Samuel, "Joey, help me get the rope out my bag, so we can toss it down."

Joey helped me tie some rope together and then we tossed it down. We tied our end to a sturdy tree.

"Alright, we got it. We're coming up!"

"Thank God for Samuel!" Alice said, sitting down to take a break. We all patiently waited, and after about 10 or 15 minutes, William had climbed his way back up to us. Sam was just a few seconds behind him. Alice and Michelle ran to William, and they both asked him if he was alright and made sure he was okay.

"I'm okay, really. Samuel came down and grabbed me before I was really able to get too far down or hurt myself," William said to the girls. They both were covered in mud, and they smelt like straight garbage.

"Thank you, Sam. You're a real life saver," Michelle said to Sam.

"Just doing my job," he said, wiping some of the mud off his body. I grabbed Sam by his shoulder, gave him a head nod, and said thank you again. He then grabbed all his things and started leading us back through the jungle like nothing happened. We kept on going; William continued to wipe the mud off, and Joey changed his spot in the line because walking behind William was no longer an option because of the way he smelled. Besides the heat burning us completely to death, the smell was probably the second worst thing about this jungle. Well, these bugs kept buzzing in my ear and touching my face; that was a huge problem as well. So that actually might be the second worst thing. It was like the insects were purposely trying to piss me off.

Samuel continued on to lead us, but I noticed we all had been complaining nonstop since we arrived here at the island. Michelle complained about her hair and the sweating; Alice about her feet, Joey about everything, myself about the heat, and lastly William about the mud and the way it's making him smell. Just complaining every step of the way. Like a bunch of bad children. I could tell it was pissing Sam off, but I kept complaining like everyone else.

As we went on, we continued to complain, but also we were passing up land marks and signs that we were getting closer to the flower. Now we had only been walking through this jungle for a few hours today and were already so close to the center. Clearly we all knew this wasn't a large island by any means, but I didn't think we'd get to the center so fast. I was just a little relieved because we were getting so close. I couldn't take this jungle any more—it was killing me.

The line stopped moving. Then a voice grazed over us from the front of the pack saying, "Alright, let's take a break." It was Samuel who spoke.

We were in a pretty wide-open area. Of course, surrounded by trees, but branches and leaves weren't constantly smacking me in the face and mouth. Leader Samuel just leaned against a tree and watched us. The girls sat their gear down and sat on a log. I stood over by them and rested for a second. Joey and Will were a little further back, so once they got to where the rest of us were Joey dropped to the ground started drinking whatever water he had left. William tried to come next to us, but he still smelled from the mud.

"Hold on Will. You're still our friend, but don't come any closer. You stink," Michelle said politely.

We all laughed a little, and William replied, "Alright yeah that's fair. As long as we're still friends, it's all good with me."

Joey pulled out a little white cloth and wiped his face and neck. The cloth was double sided now with one side being black and brown. The shade of his dirty sweat caught him off guard because he just sat there looking at it for a second.

"Eew, Joey that's disgusting," Alice said.

"I bet if I was to wipe your ass with it, the cloth would burn. We're in a jungle, so relax, sweetheart," Joey snapped back.

"I don't understand why you have to be such a dick, Joey," Michelle added in.

"What are you talking about, love? She came at me she asked for that. You always got something to say. Always running your mouth!"

"Joey, you need to calm down and shut the shit up!" William said in his angry (deep) voice.

"Either you're complaining or you're arguing. Do you people ever just talk? Or do anything else," Samuel said as he walked away for a minute, mumbling in anger in a different language.

"And I don't know what the hell he's talking about. We're complaining about his shitty-ass boat and this stupid hot weather," Joey said angrily to himself.

"In all seriousness, don't go at Sam like that, because for one he does have a point and he has done nothing but help us since we met him," William said from afar because he still stunk.

"No, he helped you because you fell and almost died. Other than that, he has been doing what we pay him to do," Joey said standing back up.

"I don't even know why you waste your time talking to him, Will. He doesn't listen to anyone," Michelle said looking at Joey.

"Come on, guys, we're supposed to be a team. Let's start making an effort to start acting like we like work together at least? Sam is right. Why do we always have to argue with one another? We've been working with each other for years. It's time we start acting like it." I stepped in and said. Everyone was quiet for a minute or two.

"I'll be friends with all of you once we find the flower and get back home." Alice said ringing the sweat out her shirt. Everyone laughed and Michelle said, "Amen to that sister. All of this will be worth it once we get the Magin flower."

"I know you guys think I'm doing this for fame or whatever but can you all just be real with me for a minute and admit this is Nobel Prize worthy? Like it or not were going to be famous for this."

I started to smile pretty hard because for once I believed him.

"Yeah, Joey, you might be right about that, but we are really doing it to help people in need," Alice responded looking at William. I looked at Will, and he put his head down and turned to face the other way. I knew that last one got to him, so I decided to change the direction of the conversation away from hitting his dad.

"Hey guys, I just wanna thank you all for joining me on this adventure (trying not to laugh), because you didn't have to and I got to say...." (I paused for a second.) "We might be the smartest, bravest people on the planet."

"You got that right! Whoa. (Laughing)" Michelle said, high fiving Alice.

"I agree with that. Let me get some of that action!" Joey said, throwing his hand out in the air looking for a high five. He stood there leaning in with his hand out and a stuck smile just waiting for one of the girls to reward him with a high five. The high five never came, and he got mad and said, "Come on I thought we all was cool now. Our leader just gave us that brief pep talk, so I thought we're all on the same page. I bet if William wanted a high five, you'd give it to him."

"Yes, you are correct. I happen to like Will," Alice said laughing with Michelle.

"But I'm the asshole, right?" Joey said, shaking his head and looking at me. Samuel had come back, and we all knew it was time to get going again. Everyone had that look of disappointment, and before he could tell us to get moving, we all started gathering our things with bad attitudes. And just like little soldiers, we all fell back in line and started walking again.

Since we were walking in a single file line, Michelle was behind Samuel, followed by Alice. I was behind Alice, and I thought I saw something crawling (upwards) on her backpack. It was really hot, and I could have just been seeing things. I rubbed my eyes and walked a little closer to get a better look. It looked like a big fuzzy hand was crawling up her back. Then it hit me.

"Oh my gosh! Alice, there's a spider on your back!" I yelled. She dropped her bag and gear immediately. The spider was too big for me to smack or take off of her. She must have felt it touch her skin because then she really started moving. She was shaking her hands up and down, screaming from the top her lungs and running in place. Nobody else helped (mainly because none of us knew what to do or wanted to touch the spider), in fact Samuel slowly walked back toward her and watched her shout for a few more minutes. Michelle and William didn't know what to do because they didn't see a spider, and I didn't see one either once she started going berserk.

"What the hell is wrong with you, Alice?! Get a damn grip!" Joey yelled. I guess he didn't hear me yell spider a few minutes ago, but more than likely he did, and he was just being a dick hole as usual.

"(Screaming) I feel it! I feel it on me! (Screaming) Sweet Christ, I feel it! Somebody do something!" Alice cried as she continued shout and freak out.

"Alright! Alright, Alice. You need to calm down. Just relax and calm down," William said walking closer with his hands up (like he was actually going to help and do something). Samuel grabbed Alice's shirt and yanked it off real quick, then a shook the shirt and a giant tarantula fell out. Everyone jumped back and gasped loudly at the same time. Samuel pulled out a small knife from his side and stuck the spider right in its back.

"Thank you very much, but can I please have my shirt back? Or what's left of it?" Alice asked. He tossed her the shirt back and placed the spider under his boot, then stepped on it slowly so that we could hear all its bones snap under his boot.

"That (light pause) was (light pause) gross," Michelle said, balling up her face with disgust. Alice picked up her bag, and we started following Samuel again. Joey was behind me in line and whispered to me, "How long did you think Tarzan was gonna let Alice dance around like one of these jungle monkeys before he killed that spider?"

Before I answered him, I thought about what he said. It was strange on how long he let that go on. Also we had been complaining and pissing him off since we got to the island, but that was still no excuse. So that was something to think about.

"I'm not sure, but I'm glad he killed the thing though," I answered.

"Well, if you ask me, the dudes a cock." I wanted to laugh at what he said because it was kind of funny, but I couldn't support him in that statement because he (Joey) was a cock.

"Well, it's a good thing I'm not asking you then," I said, back ending the conversation. We continued on, and it seemed like the jungle got hotter. This jungle was specifically designed to kill me. Alice and Michelle were up front to help show Samuel which direction we needed to go in because they had the maps (at least we were consistently getting closer). After seeing that hairy eight-legged beast on Alice every five seconds, I was checking myself and patting myself down for spiders and bugs. Of course, when we were first planning this trip, I was thinking about snakes. Now I don't know for sure, but I bet William was thinking about it, too, because we watched movies like anaconda, where the snakes were devouring people whole. So, snakes were clearly on my fear list for this trip. But thankfully we hadn't encountered any. Didn't plan on coming across any either.

"This is ridiculous! How much further, man? Can't take this shit anymore, my God." Joey yelled from the back of the pack.

"Just a few more minutes," I replied lying back.

"No, man. Enough is enough. I can't do another few more minutes," Joey moaned back.

"Please stop it with the complaining," Samuel said from the front of the pack. Samuel stopped instantly! Everyone stopped, and we all paused for a second. Samuel moved his head slowly from side to side looking around. We all were scared to ask what was wrong. It seemed like the jungle was completely still. It went silent, too; only the sound of us breathing filled the air. In a blink of an eye, a figure leaped out the trees beside us with a loud roar! Everyone screamed and took off running.

My heart was pounding against my chest, and without thinking I was running for my life. Over the sound of the girls screaming, I could hear Will repeatedly saying, "Oh shit oh shit oh shit!" over and over again as he passed everyone up. Everyone was running through and around the tress. I have never been more afraid in my life. I looked back behind me, and it was a black panther! Joey was trying to stay in front of the beast, but it was gaining on him.

"Samuel, do something for fuck's sake!" Joey yelled. Samuel was towards the front of the pack, but he turned around and pulled out a gun that he had hidden. I kept running but only a few seconds after he turned around. I heard four gun shots. More gun shots followed, and in the corner of my eye Michelle tripped and slammed into the ground. I stopped and tried to help her back up. It looked like Alice and Will kept running, but can you really blame them? As I tried to help her up, she screamed when standing on her left ankle. We both knew it was at least sprained or broken. Gunshots were firing in the background.

"Please don't leave me," she said staring into my eyes with the feeling of disappear. I looked up, and Samuel was running in between trees still shooting at the black beast. As Samuel dueled with the devil, I placed her arm around my neck and supported her weight on me. We started making our away from the danger.

Joey ran past us and yelled, "Come on! Let's go!"

"How about some help then?" I replied still walking toward him. Joey looked behind us and saw Samuel and his duel with the panther and took off running again.

"Son of a bitch," Michelle whispered after seeing Joey take off. She kept trying to pick up her speed. Michelle and I turned to look back, and Samuel was laying down against a tree but the panther was gone. Nothing but a trail of blood that led and disappeared into the thick jungle. I told her that we could make it, and she started crying. We kept moving. We continued to make our way through the jungle, and we saw everyone just standing there. They didn't seem freaked out or anything.

"Guys, we have to keep moving! What's wrong with...?" Before I was able to finish what I wanted to say I had walked up to them and saw what they was staring at. It was the drop, 100 feet wide, and a straight drop down into the cave that housed the Magin flower. It was like nothing else mattered. We found the cave. Joey picked up a rock and dropped it down the dark abyss. After a few seconds, we heard a splash.

"We need to go back first and make sure Samuel is alright," I said, setting Michelle down.

"Fuck that! For what? We're here, Dillon, we made it. We can go down there and get what we came for," Joey said strongly while pointing into the dark hole.

"And then what?! We need him to guide us back to the boat!" I yelled back.

"Look, Dillon, is right. We'll get Sam and come right back here," Will added in. Alice stayed quiet. She just kept looking into the pit.

"Alice can stay here with me while you guys grab Sam and come back here," Michelle said holding her ankle.

"How about I stay here, and you guys go and grab Samuel!" Joey replied back at Michelle.

"No, Joey! She's right. We need to go back and get him. We'll come right back here," I said, turning my attention back toward Joey.

Will grabbed my arm and said, "Come on. Let's get Sam and get back here. Let all the women stay together."

It didn't feel right leaving him with them, but we needed to get Sam. Will and I started walking back. This time, we were always checking around and constantly looking behind us. When we got to Samuel, he was still breathing but had a huge claw marks going across his stomach. The panther must have scratched him pretty good. He was covered in blood. The dark red life lightly made its way out his mouth. His hand pressed softly on the claw mark too big for his hand to cover. Will and I tried to carry him back to the others, but with every step we took, he lost more blood. It was getting harder and more point-less to carry him.

"We have to stop this bleeding before we go any further," Will said as he tore off a piece of his clothing off and wrapped it around Sam's body. Sam tried to say something, but I told him to save his energy before he could get it out. I knew there was a man losing his life right in front of me, but I could not stop thinking about the flower. I mean, we actually found it. All we had to do was climb down into the drop and swim to the cave. The flower should be down there, and we could climb out and head back to the boat. Five days in this jungle of hell had fi-nally paid off!

"Dillon! Dillon! Jesus, man. I've been calling you for like five minutes. Help get him back to the others," I heard Will yelling as I was snapping out of it and coming back to my senses. We got him back, and it looked like Alice had wrapped up Michelle's ankle, and Joey and set up all the climbing gear. Joey was ready to go down and hooked up the rest of the equipment.

We put Sam down, and Joey said, "Well if you two don't mind I would like go down and get this flower, so we can get out of here."

Will and I knew we should go down now because Alice started putting on the harness to go down. When Alice was ready to go down, then we really knew to gear up and head down. We had no choice but to leave Samuel until we returned. Michelle stood and started putting on her harness.

"No way. You should sit this one out. You cannot go down there on that ankle," I said trying to take her rope away from her.

"No! I have traveled too far and did too much to not do go down. Like it or not, I'm coming," she answered back, snatching the rope out my hands.

"Fine, but stay close to me."

We were all set and ready to go down into the pit. Everyone had their gear and a helmet with a flashlight attached. We were all more than ready to go down.

And so we did. With our rope attached to an archer stuck in the ground, we slowly started walking ourselves down into the darkness. I couldn't believe we were actually doing this. Darkness filled the air around us. I kept looking at every-one, but they were focused on trying to get down.

With every step I took, it got lower, and it got darker. I could smell the water below us, and the sound of the jungle began to fade away. The light from our flash-lights carved a way through the deep black. Looking straight down into the water, I hung on the wall. The water was still and clear blue.

We reached the water, and across was the entrance into the cave. We had to swim to the entrance, but it was only about a 40-foot swim to the cave.

"Careful everyone!" Will's voice echoed throughout the pit until it made its way out.

One by one, we dropped into the water and glided across. I got there first, so I helped everyone else up onto the land. We took a second to just look around. The cold water was still sending chills through my body. I put Michelle's arm around my neck and gave her more support.

Alice walked in front of us and said, "We should keep moving; we're almost there."

As we went deeper into darkness, the walls of the cave seemed like they were moving in closer in toward us. Everyone stopped and turned around because we heard something. It sounded like some rocks had fell. A gentle breeze brushed be-tween my arms. Michelle was shivering because she was still wet. I thought we all would be more talkative, but since we started coming down into the pit, we hardly spoke. Alice was in the front, and she stopped which caused us all to. We heard the rocks again.

"What's wrong?" I asked.

The ground cracked and split open right under Alice and she dropped. The sound of her screaming frightened my soul. Will was behind her, and he dropped, too. Their voices disappeared into the fallen deep. I tried to turn Michelle and me around, so we could start running the other way, but Joey darted off and ran past us. The ground continued to crack open. Michelle was screaming in my ear and then I felt nothing under my feet. I dropped down; my heart flew up into my throat as I dropped down. Michelle grabbed onto my arm squeezing and screaming for her precious life.

"Jesus!" I moaned as we crashed into the ground, but it was at angle, so we continued to fall. Sliding down, I was trying to keep her close to me. Michelle kept on sliding, but I slammed into a rock and flipped over. I crashed into the ground and started sliding back down again. My back and legs were killing me after crash-ing into that rock. Everything started to slow down. I could hear less and less. Even the darkness faded away.

TO BE CONTINUED...

Into the Dark
will return in Volume Two

MR. CLARK DILLON JR